Jack's Divine Fruit

Written by **LISA NORMAN**

Illustrated by **VIKAS UPADHYAY**

ISBN: 979-8-9893706-3-4

Illustrated by Vikas Upadhyay
Produced by Publish Pros | publishpros.com

For Jack with all my love

But the **FRUIT** of the Spirit is love, joy, peace, patience, kindness, goodness, faithfulness, gentleness, and self-control. Against such things there is no law.

GALATIANS 5:22-23

Jack and his Mom were walking in the park one day.
Sharing their favorite things was a game they liked to play.

"Mom, let's talk about fruits, just me and you.
I'll say a **FRUIT** I really like, and then you say one too."

"All the colors and shapes," Mom said, "as brilliant as can be,
like the FRUIT of the Spirit that grows in you and me."

"I love bright red
STRAWBERRIES,
ever so juicy and sweet.

Heart-shaped with
tiny black seeds,
they're always
such a treat.

They grow on flowering plants
fairly low to the ground.
In many jams and jellies
they can often be found.

They're also in fancy desserts
that I've watched you make—
milkshakes, ice cream, and fillings
for pastries, pies, and cake."

"**LOVE** is a fruit that is boundless and very good for the heart,
a strong certain feeling, it's a great place to start.

When we love we put others' needs in front, before our own.
With love in our heart, we are never ever alone.

Showing that you care, with a big warm embrace,
tells someone you love them and makes the world a better place."

"With its thick yellow skin
and soft fruit inside,
BANANAS are delicious
fresh, cooked, or dried.

Just a few brown spots
makes the texture just right.
I can hardly wait
to take the next sweet bite!

Rich in fiber and potassium,
it grows on a tall tree,
but if its peel is still green…
it's not quite ready for me!"

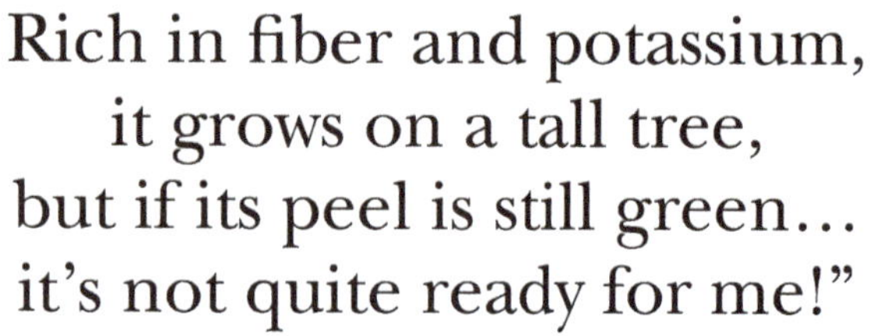

"**JOY** is a fruit that comes from somewhere way down deep,
an enduring presence of peace to treasure and keep.

When you spread joy and cheer, it grows in bunches, you will see.
Sharing happiness is a gift, like bananas from the tree.

Choose happiness every time even when things get tough.
The joy of the Lord is our strength, and that is always enough."

"The **PEACH** is orange-yellow
with velvet skin indeed,
and a shell of hard wood
that envelops its seed.

They are ripe when they are soft,
no longer firm to the touch.
The flavors dance on your tongue,
which I enjoy very much.

They smell as good as they taste,
both tangy and sweet.
With a piece of peach cobbler,
your dinner's complete!

"**PEACE** is like peaches as they grow on trees above.
We have peace in our heart when we know we are loved.

Sitting in comfort knowing God is on our side,
we can sit back, relax and enjoy life's amazing ride.

Enjoying nature, feeling grateful, and loving ourselves too,
are how we nurture the inner peace that grows in me and you."

"**PINEAPPLES** are a large oval fruit
with rough, prickly skin,
and delicious yellow flesh
that lies just within.

Grown in warm tropical places
its sweet taste will thrill.
Pineapple flavors a smoothie
or can even be grilled.

You can judge the ripeness
by examining its spikes.
Hawaiian-style pizza
is my very favorite type."

"You need **PATIENCE** for pineapples to grow, I've learned.
Take patience to the playground as you wait your turn.

Show grace to others, forgive mistakes they've had.
Don't give way to anger if someone makes you mad.

Don't be in a rush. Let others take their time.
Have mercy and compassion, and things will work out fine."

"**ORANGES** are citrus fruits
that grow on certain trees.
They have small white flowers
and beautiful shiny leaves.

A tough vibrant skin
holds together many sections,
peeled or squeezed for juice,
it's one of my favorite selections.

The goodness of an orange
is something to behold.
Packed with Vitamin C,
they can help you fight a cold!"

"You must stand up for **KINDNESS** wherever you may go.
When you do you should find a beautiful grove will grow.

Being kind involves sharing and treating people with respect.
Helping to lift up others is a trait to never neglect.

Let a heart full of grace always shine through,
and know a kinder world can start with just you."

"**APPLES** are crisp and crunchy.
This everyone knows.
Each has a dimple on the top,
from where the stem grows.

They turn red, yellow, or green
each and every fall,
and the Honeycrisp kind
is my favorite of all.

An apple a day is good for you.
They're rich in Vitamin C.
They are ever so tasty
and the juice is so sweet."

"**GOODNESS** grows in our hearts like apples on the tree.
Following the rules makes you the best that you can be!

Showing love to others makes your heart expand.
It also feels really good to lend a helping hand.

You make the right choices. You're the 'apple' of my eye.
The power of true goodness is something we can't deny."

"**BLUEBERRIES** are a small fruit
and very nutritious.
Rich in antioxidants,
they are simply delicious!

Soft plump ones are sweet
and the tiny ones tart,
Fresh blueberry muffins
always win over my heart.

They are a superfood
I like to eat every day,
whether as a snack at school
or as frozen sorbet."

"**FAITHFULNESS** is being dedicated to those we hold dear,
like God is faithful to us daily and year after year.

Just like all of your favorite fruits that start out as seeds,
our faithful God takes care of us and all of our needs.

These delicate berries teach us about God's generosity too.
He provides food that sustains us, always loyal and true."

"**WATERMELONS** are giant fruit
that look like they could burst.
They have a thick green rind
and will always quench your thirst.

Their slightly bitter flavor
keeps the sweet part at bay.
They are the best part of a picnic
on a hot summer day.

Watermelons have a unique texture
and may have some seeds too,
even the white part of the rind
is surprisingly good for you!"

"**GENTLENESS** is something that spreads slowly over time,
like watermelons sprawling along a trailing garden vine.

Be tender, calm, and humble in all the things that you do.
Mildness and meekness show the fruit of gentleness in you.

Give hugs freely to let friends know you are always there.
Lift them up and bless their life by showing them you care."

"Tight red and green bunches of
GRAPES grow on the vine.
Cotton candy flavor
is a favorite of mine.

With a slight crunchy texture
and dry, sweet-tarty taste,
on fancy cheese boards you'll see grapes
decoratively placed.

Use them as a garnish.
Grow an arbor you walk through.
Try them frozen as icy treats.
They have health benefits too!"

"Just as the smallest grapes become large clusters on a vine,
little bits of **SELF-CONTROL** can add up over time.

Always show others love. Think before you act or speak.
Avoid temptation when in doubt and the right path you'll seek.

Watch your role models and hear what they have to say.
Self-control develops as you listen and obey."

These **FRUITS** require a lot of sunlight, water, and care.
They are constant reminders that God is always there.

We are planted in His heart because of His deep love, you see,
and as we love Him in return, His fruit grows in you and me.

No matter what fruits you choose or your favorites are to taste,
they are all a part of God's Garden, grown with amazing grace.

God, the perfect vinedresser, knows just what each of us needs.
We produce luscious fruit for His glory by doing good deeds.

The Fruit of the Spirit is not like the other fruit we eat.
Instead, it's fruit that feeds our souls, that shows us who to **BE**!

As His spirit works in us, our fruit pleases God above,
a harvest of righteousness blossoms to honor His great love.

Seek the light of God's love everywhere you go,
and you will be anchored in good soil and continue to grow.

As the world hungers for this fruit, we lean on Him and pray.

God's love grounds our lives and gives us strength each day.

We are rooted in God's grace, every boy and girl,
so go forth and share His divine fruit with the world.

Author Lisa Norman

Dr. Lisa Norman was born and raised in Dalton, in beautiful northwestern Georgia. Lisa considers her faith and family to be most important to her. She is the wife of a financial advisor, mother of four children, and a practicing physician. She is passionate about the arts, especially piano and all forms of dance, and as a former exchange student in both Argentina and Spain she has a special interest in Hispanic cultures. Her love for writing poetry began at an early age and has continued throughout her life. A graduate of Wake Forest University and Emory School of Medicine, Lisa lives with her family in Winston Salem, North Carolina.

Learn more at LisaNormanBooks.com.